Samuel Jackson Pratt

Landscapes in Verse

taken in spring

Samuel Jackson Pratt

Landscapes in Verse
taken in spring

ISBN/EAN: 9783337369132

Printed in Europe, USA, Canada, Australia, Japan

Cover: Foto ©Andreas Hilbeck / pixelio.de

More available books at **www.hansebooks.com**

LANDSCAPES

IN VERSE.

TAKEN IN SPRING.

BY

THE AUTHOR OF SYMPATHY.

THIRD EDITION.

LONDON:

PRINTED FOR T. BECKET, PALL-MALL.

M,DCC,LXXXV.

ARGUMENT.

Abſence of CLEONE :——Its Effects on THEODORUS, an Enthuſiaſt.——The Imagery chiefly ſought by, and moſt deſirable to, ſeparated Lovers.—Addreſs to the Muſes.—Invocation to FANCY:——Her Power variouſly illuſtrated;—Favours THEODORUS by painting CLEONE as preſent.—LANDSCAPES:—Morning; ——the Cliff——the Mountain——the Mead——the Style——the River——the Orchard——the Cottage and Cottagers——the Fir-Grove——the different Objects and Scenery deſcriptive of and belonging to each.——AGENOR and FANNY, an Epiſode.——Sunſhine and Cloud:—Happineſs and Miſery.—THEODORUS continues his Landſcapes——The Lake, &c. &c.——The Power and Influence of the Lyre upon the Imagination and the Paſſions:—Ambition—Revenge—Jealouſy—Genius—Friendſhip and Love—Conſolatory Ode; &c. &c.

LANDSCAPES

IN VERSE.

CLEONE loſt!—though loſt but till the moon,

On her blue throne with creſcent ray ſhall ſhine,

(O ſpace eternal to th' enamour'd heart!)

Young THEODORUS,—of his paſſion proud,

And fondly nurſing ev'ry woe it brings,

Proud of the ſacred lyre,—Affection's friend—

Sorrow and Love's aſſociate—from the world

Withdrawn—thus tun'd th' enthuſiaſt lay.——

B   Sun

Sun, veil thy beams! nor with unwelcome light

Pierce the deep folitude my foul has found

Sacred to Love, to Silence, to CLEONE.

Arch over arch let woven verdure fpread:

Thicken thy darkeft foliage round my bower,

O Nature, Goddefs of this green recefs!

Folly, obtrude not on my virtuous fighs,

Sighs, from which Folly ever muft be free,

For when did Folly love? or when fhall know

The cherifh'd Grief that fhuns fociety,

Feeds on her faithful tears, and finds a charm,

Where Folly fears to tread, but Love delights

(In abfence of the nymph ador'd) to dwell.

Paffion's pale haunts, all hail!—The foreft glooms,

Whofe tenfold umbrage midft the blaze of noon

Sheds utter darknefs:—The chill cell of Him,

Who holds no farther converfe with the world:—

The cavern'd rock, which opes its fhaggy jaws

Befide the main, to drink the foaming wave:—

The hut of fhepherd on the blafted heath,

Where Pleafure's eye turns frighted from the wafte,

And the keen winds, which here find no controul,

Tear up the hardy Thiftle by its root,

Tho' native of the defert:—The feath'd tree,

Black with the pafling lightnings:—The deep dell

Bufhy and unfrequented, where the ftreams

Work their flow paflage thro' the tangled brook:—

The cyprefs grove:—The church-yard guarding yews

Waving o'er recent graves, ev'n while the moon

Shines on the graffy bed of mouldering friend,

Where

Where oft we chill our bofoms with the dews

That bathe his turf:—The fudden-opening tomb

That fhews to Fancy's eye the fhivering form,

Dead and alive at once, of her who late

Fill'd our bereaved arms :——Paffion's pale haunts,

Again, all hail!——

          Here THEODORUS paus'd,

But foon to Melancholy's fofter note,

Suiting his lyre, th' attemper'd ftrain began.

Ah me! with what a leaden pace the hours

Lag on, retarding with their cumbrous wings,

When firft divided from the nymph we love!

Yet fleeter than the tracklefs lightning's flame,

Speed the quick minutes when we court their ftay ;

And ere th' impaffion'd vow, at morning feal'd

On fair CLEONE's lip, can be enfhrin'd

Upon my heart, Love's faithful regifter,

The warning watch-bell from yon jealous tower,

Tolls out the parting knell.   But now, alas!

Ah! that his pinion fafter than the light

Could poft to our next meeting!—Surly Time

Acrofs his fhoulder hangs the vacant fcythe

Upon his idle crutch fufpended leans,

And with the lingering ftep of ftooping age

Lengthens each flagging moment to a year!

Come then, ye Mufes, forrow-foothing Maids,

Ye who can pencil high the future joy!

Come, with Imagination's pregnant ftore

Of

Of young ideas, tender-tinted flowers

Of fragrance heavenly fweet, and hue divine,

Come, with foft Confolation :—O, defcend,

And bring along, companion ever-lov'd

Fancy—the brighteft of th' ætherial hoft,

She, who in vifionary robes of light,

Sky-woven, and of texture exquifite,

Finer than threaded fun-beams—know'ft to drefs

Anew, that parted blifs, which in the urn

Of yefterday was clos'd; fhe who revives

What Time has torn away ; who can reftore

The dead,—the buried—fuch is tranfport loft:—

Blefsed enchantrefs! who by Mem'ry's aid

Canft bid the raptures of the *paft* arife,

Unblemifh'd from the tomb, in all their charms.

Fancy, attend! for thou, magician fair,

The angel form of her my foul adores,

Canft place before my eyes. And foft: methinks,

Led on by thee, I have her in my view;

Lo! there her gracious image! we trace back,

By thee affifted, O feraphic guide!

Each hallow'd ftep to recollection dear:

And tho' the fpace of many a gloomy league

Cruel divides me from her gentle hand,

Benignant Thou haft lock'd it faft in mine,

And bids it give me back the thrilling touch

That fpeaks a kind return; or lays it foft

Upon the breaft which fcarcely holds the heart,

That in fweet tumult trembles at the preffure.

And

And now, again, by thy celeftial power

We tafte together morning's balmy gale,

And dafh the early dew-drop from the thorn;

We mark the maiden verdure of the fpring

Juft burfting from the buds—her violets cull

Where blue they bloom in fair humility—

Emblems of virgin grace and modeft worth—

The lovelieft tenants of the lowlieft hedge

Yet fweeter than the proudeft flower, that grows,

Child of ambition, on the mountain's top.

Now flow along the bloffom'd dale we go

Wooing fequefter'd Silence, where fhe fits

Embow'r'd with fhrubs (impervious to the ken

Of eyes which keep their worfhip for the world)

Refuge

Refuge of tender hearts, who ftill muft fear

(So delicately white th' unfullied glofs

Of innocence in love and faith engag'd)

To " fpot its fnowy mantle,*" fhould it mix

With the mad multitude, where paffions fell,

And ftrangers to their bofom, enter wild,

Like Sin and Death in Paradife, to jar

On the foft mufic of according fouls!

Together now we climb th' afpiring brow

Of yonder tow'ring cliff, where zephyrs bland

Come frefh from heav'n to greet us:—there arriv'd,

Ev'n at the fkyey fummit, far from men

And near the breath of Gods, we reft awhile;——

* Sterne.

Ah! pause to memory precious; grac'd, perchance,

With ev'ry fond endearment honeft Love

Dare afk, or innocent Affection give :——

The joy of admiration undifturb'd ;—

The ardent gaze of fondnefs o'er the face

That blooms a thoufand graces on the look,

As deep attention draws the varying blufh ;—

The thrilling glance, that in the trembling heart

Stirs the deep figh, and pierces ev'ry fenfe

With aching rapture Love alone can feel ;—

The touch which holieft Innocence allows,

A touch, tho' lighter than the goffamer,

Or the thin down that from the thiftle flies

When fummer zephyrs fport, can fhake the frame

More than the hurricane the bending reed ;—

The

The faultering accent;—Paffion's lavifh praife,

Ah! gracious Flattery!—Silence too, that pleads

Beyond what Tully fpoke—an eloquence

Unborrow'd of the tongue, which every heart

In love interprets, feels conviction ftrong,

That language never yet (tho' breath'd from lips

Where Science dwelt, and Harmony her feat

Had fix'd, to win and to inform the ear)

Could boaft—the filent Eloquence of Love.

Again he paus'd : again renew'd the fong.

But foft! methinks we now delighted trace

The varied beauties of the vale below,

Where art and nature rival wonders give,

C 2

Each

Each prodigal of objects meet to lure

The roving eye, which travels o'er the whole.

Lo! Fancy now is seated on the hill,

To etch the vernal landscape, as it spreads

In one unbounded profpect from the bower

And neighb'ring fount, facred to Love fincere:

Ev'n there, methinks, we now together ftand

At radiant morn, charm'd with thefe varied views:

The dwindled city half conceal'd in fmoke:—

Mortals diminifh'd,—to the blufh of pride—

Hurrying like bufy emmets thro' the ftreet:—

The cultur'd gardens glittering in the dew:—

The fcarce-diftinguifh'd hufbandman, who bends

To drefs the grateful foil:—The quiet fheep

Which

Which on th' adjacent mountain feem to hang

Their fleeces on its fides:—The dufky car,

The interfecting roads, whofe whit'ning gleam

Contraft the verdure of the fmiling meads:—

The river, like a ferpent, twining fair

In many a lucid labyrinth, glowing now

With Morn's reflected beam, now fombrous made

By darkling fhadows as they flit along

Swifter than gliding fpectres:—The fmall cots,

Abodes of wholefome labour—where we fee

How few, how cheap, and eafily fupply'd

The real wants of man:—The pillar'd domes,

Abodes of wealth and grandeur—which difplay

Neceffities that nature never form'd:—

A gorgeous wafte of proud magnificence!—

And

And laſt we note the intermixing fanes,

Abodes of rapt devotion—which the ſun,

As conſcious of their ſanctity, inveſts

With orient light, that like a glory plays

Upon the holy ſpire, and ſainted tower!

Next, Fancy wanders with us down the ſlope,

In variegated blooms and verdure rich,

To yonder path, that in the bottom lies,

Which clad in tendereſt green, ſcarce ſhews the print

Of Love's light ſtep, beneath whoſe preſſure ſmooth

Springs many a flower, which in life's beaten road

Refuſe to grow, or ſhed their modeſt ſweets

Too fragrant for the world.——No ſounds are here

But low of heifer, bleat of lambkin mild,

Matin

Matin of warbling bird, or lapfe of rill,

Whofe fcarce-heard murmur, like the tender plaint

Of fome fond youth juft parted from his nymph,

Wailing a moment's abfence, fighs fo foft

'Tis tearful pleafure.   Now we view the ftile,

A fimple branch of maple plac'd aflant,

Ruftic and unadorn'd; near which the May-bufh waves

Its virgin bloffoms, while beneath its fhade

Wild flow'rs, in love with water, faintly lend

Their fcanty effence, bathed in the brook

Which, by the foot-ftone, trickles to the verge

Of the fair river, who with eafy flow

Glides filent on, and oft, in paffing, greets

His aged willows, that in waiting feem

To bow their bare and venerable heads

Along

Along his tufted banks. Ah! fpot ferenc!

Here by the various charm of nature bound,

Each object ftealing fwift into the heart,

By potent Truth impell'd, by Fancy fir'd,

Soften'd by Love, by all in union met,

That fills the eye with Paffion's blifsful tear,

The breaft with tranfport, and the foul with joys,

Which few of this bad world, alas! fhall feel,

CLEONE tries her pencil, fketching fair

The Paradife fhe fhares:—The landfcape lives

Beneath her magic touch:—And lo! the glen

Skirting the lucid ftream, where flow'ring fhrubs,

The hawthorn hedge, and many an orchard tree,

Whofe antique trunks, with moffy coats are wrapt,

While from their arms, irregular and old,

Burfts

Burfts the young bloffom, like the ruddy bloom

That temperance fixes in the wholefome cheek

Of blamelefs age:———Soft peers, thro' foliage deep,

The ruffet dwelling of an antient pair,

Who thrice ten fmiling years, beneath its roof,

(Blufh gay and great ones of a jarring world!)

Have led a virtuous life of wedded Love!

In days of nuptial diffonance and ftrife,

This pattern, rare and high, CLEONE views,

And plucking foft the unadorned latch,

Enters the cot, where love with nature reigns

Far from the city artifice:—the pair

We find, with all their progeny around,

In goodly rows affembled at the board

Of buxom health, who fpreads the light repaft,

Which

Which hofpitality, '(fuch as of yore

Our Antient Britons, lov'd, ere courtier pomp

The once wide opening door infidious clos'd)

With importunings fweet, invites to fhare.

Their offer'd boon accepted, we furvey

Silvan Simplicity her graces lend

To clear Content, who in the herdfman's hut

(Which fcorns the gilding of felicity)

Refides with real Happinefs a friend,

Ev'n as an Houfhold Goddefs, ever near

With gentle hand, to blefs this couple blythe,

To pour the fpirit of the frefheft gale

Upon the modeft rofe that humbly blows

Around their dwelling fmall:—from the clean fpring

That lends its little tide, the pureſt ſtream

To draw, for uſe or pleaſure:—o'er the couch

To ſhed the ſweeteſt ſleep from night till morn,

Light as the ſilent dews that fall in both.

And now we liſten to the honeſt tale

Of cottage fondneſs, and of cottage faith

Told by the matron, while the ſhepherd ſwain

(Inſtructed well to read the ſecret heart)

Traces with ſkill, even to its roſy ſource,

The crimſon fluſh that paints CLEONE's cheek,

As, by the ſcene ſubdued, I ſeem more cloſe

To fold her tender form:—This counſel kind

Diſtill'd at length like honey from his lip:

" Yes, youth and maiden, I can ſee yonr hearts

" Twine round each other like your circling arms:—

" Behold! in us, a pair grown old together,

" Our morning tender, and our evening true;

" Then live and love, as we have lov'd and liv'd;—

" Go with our mutual blessing on your heads;

" And when in richer domes, ye see pale Care

" Lift her proud crest to cheat the gaping croud

" With specious shews of rapture, seldom found

" In palace or in hut—then softly say,

" As many a year remote when we are laid

" Beneath the verdant turf, ye hither come,

" Here dwelt the COUPLE OF THE COT;—here oft

" We sat us down in courtship's blooming hour,

" And swore, if Hymen e'er should join our hands,

" To live as faithful, and to love as long."

All thefe, and yet a thoufand more, of power

To charm the fond enthufiaft, Fancy lends:—

And now again fhe bears us on her wings,

Gloffy with dyes, more vivid than the hues

Which in the rainbow vary, to frefh fcenes.

Under her guidance, foon, fecure we reach,

Ah! fweet remembrance! yonder breezy down

Stretch'd like a lawn, full many a verdant rood

Of velvet fod compos'd;—hard by a grove

Of all-enduring firs, their ample rows

Extend in fair array;—thither we fpeed,

There woo the umbrage, whofe immortal leaves

Outlive the wintry blaft;—along the grafs

Unfunn'd, of darkeft green, and hung with dew

That chills the length'ning glade, penfive we go,

Penfive, yet pleas'd; for gentle Love attends

Our pilgrim fteps: and where Love deigns to lead,

Smooth is the rock, and midnight darknefs fmiles.

　　At length upon a feat of mofly ftone

Refting, we liften to the whifper'd gale

That fighs amongft the trees;—lo! now it plays

On my CLEONE's cheek, or fportive hides

In her luxuriant treffes, meriting

Th' ætherial vifitant;—and hark! we hear

Another gueft afforted to the fcene,

The widow'd Turtle mourns amongft the boughs,

That echo to her fobs; and from the vale

The village bell with melancholy found

Rings

Rings out the knell of death:—at every paufe

The difmal tone admits, my throbbing heart

Suggefts to Fancy's ftartled ear, the hour,

When fhe who is now feated by my fide

(On the due motion of whofe wholefome pulfe

My being hangs) fhall wake a note like this!

O as I turn affrighted thought this way,

Horror its icy tear upon my cheek

Congeals; I draw the object of my griefs

More near my breaft, on which the laft cold drop

Of my CLEONE's life appears to fall,

And the foft orbs, which now their gentle beams

Lambent with love, dart on my inmoft foul

The light of tendernefs, fhall fhine no more.

Alas!

Alas! the blood that feeds my mourning heart

Seems wrefted from its courfe:—Strange fhudders feize

My lab'ring frame, and in *her* fate, my own

Glooms in dark characters upon my brow:

CLEONE feels the change;—and in her eye,

Of unaffected fympathy the fhrine,

Where nature's genuine incenfe fweetly flows

In fcorn of art—her imitation vile—

Springs the foft tear that hurries to her lip,

On which it hangs like dew-drops on the rofe.

I'll kifs it off.

        " O frail mortality!

" Thy flowrets bloom about the human heart

" Like flender bloffoms on the flighteft ftem

                         " Which

" Which Flora's breath may wound! ev'n as the leaf

" Of afpin young, that fhivers in the gale

" With which Aurora plays, when firft fhe fheds,

" At earlieft tinge of aromatic dawn,

" Frefh gather'd fragrance over earth and heav'n!

" Oh! of what filken texture haft thou wove

" Man's proudeft hopes! to which, the waving film

" Whofe light web floats acrofs the glowing mead,

" The radiant net-work of a fummer day,

" Is as a maffive chain, compact and ftrong!

" O frail! O weak! O poor Mortality!"

Ev'n in this felf-fame fpot, (by memory hung

With deepeft glooms)—this melancholy fpot—

E   —Now

Now many a variegated year elaps'd,

On autumn's verge and at the evening hour,

Such were the accents burfting on my ear,

As from a void—for no apparent form

Th' aftonifh'd eye that fearch'd the fcene around

Could trace——"O frail mortality!"

The breeze refum'd, in repetition ftrong,

Diftinct and aweful—"Frail mortality!"

Re-echo'd thro' the hollow of the grove,

That grove, of late fo redolent of blifs,

Whifp'ring the voice of love.—At length I faw,

From the furrounding foliage rufhing forth

Into the darkeft path, a fable form

In mourning garments—his diforder'd locks

Half veil'd his vifage—vehement and loud,

Temperate

Temperate and fad, by turns, he wept, or rav'd;

Ev'n as fome ghoft had burft th' unquiet vault

Haunting the murderer. Oft he quicker ftrode,

Spurning the ground; and as he fwept along

Would rend th' oppofing branches—lafh the air

With the torn boughs, then throw them as in fcorn

Upon the founding earth—then raife his arms—

Then clench his hands in horror; till his grief,

Like fome vaft bed of waters, fathomlefs,

Flow'd filent, in the depths of agony

For clamour too profound:—'Twas dumb defpair.

Anon the paffing bell with fullen tone

Knoll'd thro' the firs:—the falling fhades of night

Began to thicken round:—the fwelling winds

Bore the dead notes upon their viewlefs wings

Piercing

Piercing the man of forrow, who aghaft

Broke fhort his ftep, and, as by light'ning fmote,

Stood fix'd, with palms uplifted:—with foft voice

I fpake—he heard not—with a gentle ftep

I crofs'd his path—his eyes were bent on heav'n:—

He faw me not—his vifion was above!——

And next appear'd, winding th' eventful avenue,

Neareft the church-way, a fepulchral train

Amidft the torches light; which to the view

Difclos'd a coffin, whofe deep-folded pall

Six weeping damfels held, while fix fad youths

Beneath, in fable robes, their burthen bent,

Noting the funeral of fome gentle maid,

Like the fweet fnow-drop, earlieft child of fpring,

By the firft gale, untimely fwept away.

The

The man of forrow faw, and fhudd'ring fell.

Ev'n at the bare foot of yon aged tree,

The wither'd monument that marks the fcene.

The ftranger lay, cold as the corpfe he mourn'd,

That corpfe fo lov'd, fo honour'd, fo deplor'd!

But O! if thou canft pity, hear the tale:

If thou canft love, give to th' hiftoric mufe

Thy lift'ning foul, while fhe in anguifh paints

Thy changeful day—" O frail mortality!"

In FANNY's form, the graces of her heart

Were painted fair: her beauty and her worth,

Each of excelling kind, were all her dow'r:

To fortune born, and not of humble birth.

Birth, fortune, and the summer friends they bring,

The fools they buy, or flatteries they bribe,

By the strong arm of sharp adversity

That on her father prefs'd, were all deftroy'd:

A narrow cottage, and an ample foul,

That would a palace fill with generous deeds,

Were now her fire's poffeffions—fave a wife,

Choice of his youth, and honour of his age,

That grac'd his filver hair—fave this fair maid,

Pledge of their mutual faith, their mutual joy;

Who like a precious gem, from ocean fav'd,

Amidft the general wreck, with virtuous hand

Lin'd the parental couch with filial down .

More white, more foft, than what the cygnet drops

Upon the fummer ftream. In hope's fair May,

While

While yet the profpect fmil'd, AGENOR lov'd,

And fpoke his welcome flame:—the blooming youth

Was by the blooming maid belov'd again:—

But when he faw the fmiling profpect low'r,

And FANNY's golden hopes upon the wing

Of the dark tempeft tofs'd in defert air,

Shrunk he away?—Say, doft thou think he flew

Faft as that drenching ftorm, like the vile flave

Whofe foul for ever grovels in the drofs

That ftains the mine?—O no! he lov'd the more:

And as the chilling gale began to blow,

The clouds to gather, and the rain to pour,

He drew her nearer to his fhelt'ring breaft,

And fpread more wide the refuge of his arms.

Who ever purchas'd love, by aught but love?

Blufh,

Blulh, bankrupt gold, at what is ev'n beyond

Thy giant grafp:—He woo'd her gentle heart,

He woo'd and won it.——By their parents blefs'd,

✓ Blefs'd in themfelves, and in their love too blefs'd,—

Unfpotted love,—they wait the feftal hour,

That feftal hour all redolent with blifs,

For which young Fancy twines her faireft wreathe.

It comes, it comes! its odorous plumes prepare

To fpread abroad—for on the morrow's dawn,

(Which foon fhall fee a blufhing rival bloom

In FANNY's cheek) all things were fix'd to wed.

Ah interval of every foft excefs

The human heart can prove! fufpence divine!

Fill'd with each ardent hope and rofeate fear,

Where

Where PLEASURE meets her antient foe, meets PAIN,

With fuch unwonted fmiles upon his brow,

His temples bound with fweet-briar, to denote

As well the fragrant leaf as pointed thorn,

(Emblem of wedded blifs and mifery)

PLEASURE herfelf the myſtic garland takes,

And grants a truce, and is in league with PAIN:

So foft the figh, fo fweet the tear he brings,

When virgin Innocence by manly Truth

Is led to Hymen's altar. And ah! fee,

Behold! the meek eve, that foreruns that morn:

" Yet, yet awhile, a few thin fhades between,

" And thou art mine for ever," cried the youth.

F   Meanwhile

Meanwhile th' approving fire and aged dame

Beſtir themſelves, with all a parent's zeal,

To deck the bridals, and to dreſs the bower,

Fit to receive whom Eden might admit,

Where Raphael, with the firſt betrothed pair

Was wont to ſit in blifsful Paradiſe

Commiſſion'd from above.   The redd'ning weſt

Announc'd the ſetting ſun, and mellower tints

Painted the firmament: Sirius all day

His flaming car had driven along the ſky

With kindling rage.   But now the Breeze of eve,

From her cool grotto, ventur'd forth to dip

Her feathers in the rill, and in the air

To take her twilight circuit: as ſhe ſhook

Her humid pinions, nature felt reftor'd

Thro' all her works; for valley, hill, and ftream,

Bird, beaft, and man, the balmy effence hail'd!

Seafon of univerfal calm! all breath'd

Ambrofia.—Ah! what an hour for love—

Now almoft wedded love—to fteal unfeen

From all eyes but their own!—Such fweets to tafte,

Walk'd forth AGENOR and his deftin'd bride.

Now tell their happinefs, ye bleffed few

Who e'er have felt true paffion, felt your hearts

Beat quick with tranfport at the coming dawn,

Ev'n as ye feem to reach the deareft point

Of all your Fancy ever imag'd fair:—

O tell the extacy which now *they* fhar'd,

Beneath

Beneath the luftre of the rifing moon,

Arm wreath'd in arm, and foul to foul conjoin'd!

But who, alas! may truft the coming dawn?

Or, for the joys which Fancy paints fo fair,

Rely upon to-morrow? Who could yet

Chain up the tempeft? Who, when not a breeze

Difturbs the azure furface of the main,

Can fay, To-morrow fhall be calm?——Ah me!

The goodly hopes of earth, and air, and feas,

Are on the mercy of a moment flung;

And often—when their profpects fhine moft bright,

And the believing heart their promifes

Like nectar quaffs, eager as drinks the lark

The fun's firft ray, whille moift with morning dew—

The

The fweeping whirlwind is moft near:—It comes;

(Tears up the cherifh'd flower we fondly nurs'd

Ev'n in our bofoms, where we faw it bloom

With Hope's foft tears bedewing it) it comes,

And all is duft:—" O frail humanity !"

Lur'd by the fong of Philomel, who pour'd

Into their fouls her folitary chaunt,

(Which feem'd to mourn fome dear AGENOR loft)

The lovers wander'd long, and fighing drank

Each forrowing plaint; but as the cadence clos'd;

Homeward they wended; yet whene'er the lay,

Refponfive to the murm'ring of the ftream

That flow'd befide, renew'd the tuneful woe,

As if by fpell attracted tow'rds the fpot,

They

They linger'd on the brink—when swift the clouds

Resum'd the sultry power—a dead'ning heat

Without a sound, and night without a star,

Its raven vest and raven omens spread;

Trembling the breeze, trembling the moon withdrew:

Big, burning drops, where clashing elements,

Water and fire, (as if incorporate)

Appear'd to blend—the storm's fierce ministers,

Wild, savage winds, fell lightnings, and the powers

Of rolling thunder, their dire pastime took

In the astonish'd air.——Of nature's works

Tremendous, these, to FANNY's gentle soul

The most—her soul tho' innocent and pure

As skies without a cloud—from the dread shock

Of sulphurous combustion she shrunk appall'd.

Loud

Loud rav'd the hurricane: the firſt keen flaſh,

Shuddering ſhe ſaw deſcend in ſpiral flame,

Then mount and ſettle on AGENOR's breaſt,

Which like a comet ſtream'd:—a ſecond came,

And 'thwart his viſage ſhot a livid glare

Corſe-like and horrible to human view.

"Have mercy, heav'n," ſhe cried:—"he dies!—he dies!"

Then ſhriek'd and ran—ran whither? darkneſs wrapt

The troubled pool, ſave when at intervals,

The lightning blaz'd—AGENOR mad'ning call'd

Th' affrighted fugitive, but call'd in vain,

For ſoon a PLUNGE in the contiguous ſtream

(That ſtream ſo placid late, where zephyr bath'd)

Was heard, and next a piteous voice that plain'd

For inſtant aid:—that inſtant aid to give,

AGENOR

AGENOR dash'd into th' accurfed brook,

With piercing tone exclaiming——".God of earth,

" Of waters, and of heav'n! O help to fave

" This drowning lilly!"——Then with eager ftretch

That fhook the pool he fwam, uttering more loud

" I come, my foul, I come! O hither turn—

"' This faithful bofom be thy plank to fhore,

· " Thefe arms extended to their utmoft verge—

" Yet ah! they reach thee not—thy fafeguard fure!"

Myfterious Providence! a different way

Poor FANNY floated!—but at length, with voice

Like dying martyr's fweet, fhe faintly cried,

" Where art thou, love? alas! thy FANNY dies,

" But dies AGENOR's—on his bofom then,

" In his dear arms, O let me breathe my laft!"

Directed

Directed by the found, the youth now fprung,

Swifter than light can travel, thro' the flood;

Her fhivering form—in agony of grief,

Mix'd with faint hope, he caught, he felt the heart

Beat in thofe faithful arms—thofe faithful arms

Held, as he reach'd the bank, his FANNY's corpfe!

Then while he kifs'd the cold clay o'er and o'er,

Wild hurrying to the cot—raving, he cried,

" O that this vital warmth into *thy* frame

" Could be infus'd, my FANNY—that this air

" Which feeds *my* hated life could *thine* reftore—

" Ah! as I breathe into thy pale, pale lip,

" Re-animated Being—dead! quite dead!"—

Prone

Prone on the earth, ev'n with her lovely corpfe

In his embrace, he fell—then ftarting rofe

And hafted onward.——Frantic, to the hut

He bore his watry burthen—on the bed—

(By a fond matron's hands fo late prepar'd

To fold a virtuous pair—with flow'rets gay,

May blooms, and all the incenfe of the fpring,

Cull'd by a father's hand) frantic, he laid

This lovelier flower than ever Eden grew,

Or Paradife could boaft—frantic, he clung

Around the breathlefs body of the maid,

In death as life ador'd—and frantic ftill,

Alas! he lives—if life it may be call'd,

From fair fociety fhut out—the pride

Of man's fupremacy fhook from its feat,

Yet memory left to tremble o'er the paft:—

If *this* be life, he lives; in yonder dome

Thou may'ft behold the RUINS of AGENOR,

Ruins that afk no fetter, clank no chain:

His rage is fled—fad Melancholy's power

Has made his breaft her manfion—there fhe broods

And rears her gloomy throne—and mixes fighs,

And mingles tears, and blends her groans with his.

While Melancholy feems, alas! to love

Whom thus fhe grieves: but he, poor lucklefs youth,

Soften'd by fuffering, finds a charm in woe;

And oft he calls upon his FANNY loft,

And oft in myftic characters he carves

Her fancied image on the walls around;

Then tells how bleft he is, if chance he fhapes

From

From ftraw-made pillow, or from rufhy couch,

Some gift or garland that may fpeak his love.

Hail to the happier parents!—they are laid

In their pure graves, befide their angel child:

And feeft thou not, that He whom late we left,

At the dread found of FANNY's paffing bell,

At the dread view of FANNY's coffin'd pall,

Sunk on the bare foot of yon aged tree,

Was poor AGENOR's felf, who phrenzied fled

Ere FANNY for her laft home from the cot

Was mov'd along the firs, where firft began

Our tender tale:—O FRAIL MORTALILY!.

Yet from our tender tale this moral glean :—

Ah learn! even in the bofom of delight,

To take each proffer'd good with pious awe:

Should fair Felicity inviting hold

Her nectar'd cup full flowing to thy lip,

Let not pale Fear reject the smiling boon,

Lest evils *may* ensue—but *should* they come,

Should Hope's gay sun which suckles every flower

In life's mix'd garden, his bless'd beams withdraw,

(Even as the blossoms promise golden fruit)

O think on FANNY's and AGENOR's life;

By their try'd faith and goodness shape thine own;

Then, tho' like theirs, thy death be terrible,

As dark upon thy startled soul it strike,

HERE thou mayst suffer:—but there is NO HEAVEN,

(*And that there is, earth, skies, and deeps, declare)

* "And that there is, all nature cries aloud." ADDISON.

There

There is no GOD, if goodnefs fuch as theirs

Meet not eternal recompence above.

CLEONE footh'd, and Fancy ftill a friend,

Young THEODORUS thus purfued his lay:——

Fir-grove farewell!—for homeward now we bend

Our matin ftep, along the down-hill path

That fteals into the town: We view the wall,

Along whofe top the deathlefs laurel fhews

Its gloffy foliage, facred to the lyre.

With verdure old o'ergrown we note the gate

Of Gothic arching, mantled in the mofs,

With clinging ivy crown'd, and many a fhrub

That, fpurning culture, vegetates on ftone,

Mineral or fpar, or bloom-forbidding rock!

Sturdy companions of the barren wafte,

That artlefs bloffom where the *tender* flower,

Helplefs and delicate, would fade and die:

Like the foft nurfling lillies of the world,

That afk the mildeft foil, the gentleft breeze,

The fondeft care, and wither in the ftorm,

Which hardier plants, accuftom'd to the wild

And feafon'd to the elements of life,

Would brave.   Lo! in perfpective fair,

Contrafting yonder poplars' vivid rows,

Where well-arrang'd the vifta fhines complete,

The cluft'ring yew-trees wave the funeral branch

Of never-changing green;—while ancient oaks,

Forefathers of the fhade, their patriarch arms

Stretch

Stretch 'thwart the dell, where many a fathom down

Glooms the still lake, acrofs whofe furface dun,

Haunted by penfive water-fowl alone,

The fable moor-hen houfing in the fedge,

Or querulous fparrow of the humid reeds)

Slopes the fad willow, weeping as fhe dips,

In the dark ftream her melancholy boughs.

Amidft this varied fcenery we fit

A world within ourfelves—till forc'd at laft

To feek the city, the fair landfcape fades

Till morning blooms:——Such, FANCY, are thy gifts;

Thus thou redeem'ft remembrance of the paft,

At once delicious, dreadful, fadly dear,

Commixture ftrong of agony and joy,

Tranfcendent both, and cherifh'd both by love,

Whofe

Whofe very griefs are precious:—Take then, take

Thy vot'ry's thanks, pour'd from the fervid heart,

And in the defolate hour of abfence dear,

Be ever prefent, and be ever kind!

Nor deem, ye Maids Pierian, that I flight

Your gentle vifitations:—ye who oft,

In the drear hour of dark adverfity

Have help'd my trembling hands to tune the lyre,

And chear'd my penfive fpirit with your ftrains.

Sweet as the founds, and dulcet as the voice

Of melting love—Ye whofe ætherial harps,

Tun'd to the mufic of your native fpheres,

Oft, when the paffions blew their loudeft ftorm,

And keen afflictions roll'd their blackeft wave,

Have

Have wak'd Compaffion's pang-relieving tones,

Honied as voice of cherubim, and fmoothe

As the dove's plumage—ev'n the Dove of PEACE;

Upon whofe downy breaft, the troubled foul,

Lull'd by thy magic fong, forgets its rage,

Feels its griefs hufh'd, and finks fubdu'd to reft.

Hail! holy NINE! ye progeny of heav'n!

Daughters of Light and Love! fair as the orb

That opes the foul of day,—whofe orient beam,

With tuneful infpiration fraught, ye quaff,

O ever throbbing to your touch divine,

Which paints the veft of Spring with brighter hues,

Her lily's cup in purer white arrays,

Tinges with tenderer pale her cowflip's bell;

                                                                And

And on her rofe-buds frefher vermeil throws,

Beats my fond heart!—'Tis ye, who round the fun,

The fun your parent—bind with filial care,

A zone more radiant, and from ye the moon

Borrows a mellower tint, the air a balm

More foft, ocean a greener robe, and earth—

Thro' all her rich domain of wood and ftream,

Cloud-piercing mountain, and exuberant vale,

Fantaftic water-fall, and vaulted cave,

The glowing powers that gem her central mines,

And ev'ry flow'r which on her furface blooms—

To ye owe grace and beauty—Chief your fway

Th' obedient PASSIONS feel:—HUMANITY,

Thro' all her wond'rous mazes, to the Mufe

Heaps

Heaps tribute large and holy, catching, charm'd,

Lofty enthufiafm from her raptur'd lyre.

Rous'd by the fpirit, breathing in her fhell,

Forth from the panting heart, her votive train

With incenfe to her beauteous fhrine advance;

AMBITION, as he rufhes up the fteeps

Of tow'ring life, in pride of youthful days;

To win the warrior, or the patriot wreath,

Midway in his career fufpends his ftep,

Lift'ning the note that fwells to HONEST praife,

Then onward preffes to the funny brow,

Where Fame awaits to crown him:—Mad REVENGE,

Aw'd by the threat'ning lyre, awakes from dreams,

Where

Where his vex'd fpirit thro' the troublous night

Had tofs'd thro' feas of blood, while Murder drew

In vifion dire th' affaffin's reeking blade——

Soul-foften'd, fee he drops the inftrument,

And weeps upon the breaft he meant to ftain :—

Ev'n JEALOUSY, that maniac of the mind,

His pale lip quiv'ring to his dark intents,—

Intents which mark for death the maid he loves,—

(Haply for glance mifdeem'd, or dubious word,

Tortur'd to fenfe perfidious) fhould THY voice,

Like to th' Almighty fiat, bid the ftorm

Forbear to rage ;—O fhould thou touch the chord,

And thro' thy melting lute bid PITY breathe

Her fofteft mufic of forgiving love——

The furious youth like one entranced ftands,

Till

'Till streams of tendereft anguish o'er his cheek,.

Like gentle showers upon the with'ring shrub

Smote by the torrid beams of fultry noon,

Begin to flow, till lily'd Constancy

(That flower of Paradife while bleſs'd) adorns

The idol of his heart—and foon he flies

With fond repentance to her faithful arms.

Fir'd by th' ætherial Mufe, young Genius foars

An eagle flight to crop thy own-lov'd plant,

Where, fofter'd midft the regions of the fun,

And water'd by the confecrated ftream,

It grows to crown the favor'd bard, who wins

Thy partial fmile—O univerfal power,

'Tis thine to gild pale Poverty's chill hut,

Smooth the dark brow that glooms on wan difeafe,

Thine

Thine is the tear of woe, the fmile of joy,

Of focial life thine ev'ry gracious charm;

Untutor'd Nature, midft her favage wilds,

Carols with artlefs note thy wond'rous praife;

In friendfhip's facred bower, and in the path

Of rofy love, thy flow'rets fweet diffufe

Immortal fragrance, and immortal bloom.

Defcend then, O inhabitants of heav'n,

In all the colours of the glowing morn,

When May with fragrance fills the vernal gale!

And foft—in robes of variegated light,

Where blended tints of azure and of gold,

With many a filver clouding, forms a couch

In yonder fky, I fee the train Parnaffean,

With

With each the fymbol of her magic fway,

(Still Fancy grac'd and Honour as their chief)

Sit in affemblage fair—Lo! now they fpread

Their burnifh'd pinions, by the air upborn;

And hark! what mufic from their vocal fhell,

Floats on the downy bofom of the breeze:

NO more, fond youth the ftrains prolong,

Break off, break off, the plaintive fong;

With mandate high from fpheres above,

Our golden harps are ftrung to Love!

In ev'ry flow'r that nature blows,

Breeze that fans, and wave that flows;

On earth, in ocean, and in air,

Love is the fov'reign blifs, the univerfal prayer.

'Tis Love fuſtains the ſtarry choir,

Love is the elemental fire;

Ah! naught in thy mortality,

Nor ev'n in our eternity,

Like Love can charm, like Love can bleſs,

The ſun and ſoul of happineſs;

Love is to ev'ry Muſe allied,

Touches each tuneful chord, and ſpreads the chorus wide.

'Tis ours to waft the Lover's ſighs,

Swift to the Nymph for whom they riſe;

And gently as we ſtrike the ſtring,

Convey the Nymph's on roſy wing.

Abſence, tho' it wounds, endears,

Soft its ſorrows, ſweet its tears;

Pains that pleaſe, and joys that weep,

Trickle like healing balm, and o'er the boſom creep.

Love and Sorrow, Twins, were born

On a fhining fhow'ry morn,

'Twas in prime of April weather,

When it fhone and rain'd together;

He who never Sorrow knew,

Never felt Affections true;

Never felt true Paffion's power,

Love's fun and dew combine, to nurfe the tender flow'r,

Here ended they their chaunt—here FANCY too

Rode on the parting fun-beam: for the moon

ON HER BLUE THRONE BEGAN WITH CRESCENT RAY

To fhine, and raptur'd THEODORUS now

Saw his CLEONE fpeeding to his arms.

Thus in the abfence of his plumy love,

Tender of heart, the Turtle tunes his voice

To plainings gentle,, and the interval

Soothes with a foft confolatory fong,

While on the tow'ring tree's fupremeft bough

Waving he fits to ken his wand'ring mate:

But, lo! at length fhe cuts the blue profound

With wing precipitate and fond, while all

The glowing purple of her gloffy neck

Sun-burnifh'd glitters in the beam of day,

Then glad he gives his plumage to the breeze,

And fprings along to welcome her return.